Dear Parent:

Congratulations! Your child is taking the first steps on an exciting journey. The destination? Independent reading!

STEP INTO READING® will help your child get there. The program offers five steps to reading success. Each step includes fun stories and colorful art. There are also Step into Reading Sticker Books, Step into Reading Math Readers, Step into Reading Write-In Readers, Step into Reading Phonics Readers, and Step into Reading Phonics First Steps! Boxed Sets—a complete literacy program with something for every child.

Learning to Read, Step by Step!

Ready to Read **Preschool–Kindergarten**
• big type and easy words • rhyme and rhythm • picture clues
For children who know the alphabet and are eager to begin reading.

Reading with Help **Preschool–Grade 1**
• basic vocabulary • short sentences • simple stories
For children who recognize familiar words and sound out new words with help.

Reading on Your Own **Grades 1–3**
• engaging characters • easy-to-follow plots • popular topics
For children who are ready to read on their own.

Reading Paragraphs **Grades 2–3**
• challenging vocabulary • short paragraphs • exciting stories
For newly independent readers who read simple sentences with confidence.

Ready for Chapters **Grades 2–4**
• chapters • longer paragraphs • full-color art
For children who want to take the plunge into chapter books but still like colorful pictures.

STEP INTO READING® is designed to give every child a successful reading experience. The grade levels are only guides. Children can progress through the steps at their own speed, developing confidence in their reading, no matter what their grade.

Remember, a lifetime love of reading starts with a single step!

For my sister, who likes to go to the ocean
—J.A.

 Published in the United States by Random House Children's Books, a division of Random House, Inc., New York, and simultaneously in Canada by Random House of Canada Limited, Toronto.

www.stepintoreading.com

Educators and librarians, for a variety of teaching tools, visit us at
www.randomhouse.com/teachers

Library of Congress Cataloging-in-Publication Data
Armstrong, Jennifer.
Sunshine, moonshine / by Jennifer Armstrong ; illustrated by Lucia Washburn.
p. cm. — (Step into reading. A step 1 book)
SUMMARY: Illustrations and rhyming text follow the sun and moon as they shine on a young boy's day.
ISBN 0-679-86442-3 (trade) — ISBN 0-679-96442-8 (lib. bdg.)
[1. Sun—Fiction. 2. Moon—Fiction. 3. Stories in rhyme.] I. Washburn, Lucia, ill.
II. Title. III. Series: Step into reading. Step 1 book.
PZ8.3.A63Su 2004 [E]—dc21 2002153064

Printed in the United States of America 17 16 15 14 13 12 11 10

STEP INTO READING®

Sunshine, Moonshine

by Jennifer Armstrong
illustrated by Lucia Washburn

Random House New York

Sun shines on the mountains.

Sun shines on the sea.

Sun shines on my pillow,
and says wake up to me.

Sun shines on a seashell.

Sun shines on a rock.

Sun shines on a crab,

and on a gull,

and on the dock.

Sun shines on the lighthouse.

Sun shines on a sail.

Sun shines as it sinks
into the ocean like a whale.

Moon shines as it rises.

Moon shines as I yawn.

Moon shines as I try to catch
the fireflies on the lawn.

Moon shines on the houses.
Moon shines on the cars.

Moon shines like a night-light
up among the stars.

Moon shines on the mountains.
Moon shines on the sea.

Moon shines on my pillow,
and says good night to me.